RATS!
The Musical

Based on *The Pied Piper of Hamelin*
by Robert Browning

Lyrics by
JEREMY BROWNE

Music by
NIGEL HESS

VOCAL SCORE

Duration: c. 40-45 minutes
Libretto available from the Publishers

CHESTER MUSIC

(A division of Music Sales Limited)

CHARACTERS

Narrator
Rat Leader
Mayor (Alderman Greedy)
The Pied Piper
Crippled Boy

3 Solo Male Aldermen

Citizens of Hamelin
Rats
Council of Hamelin
Children

INDEX

1. PROLOGUE

Lyrics by
JEREMY BROWNE

Music by
NIGEL HESS

2. HAMELIN, HAMELIN

Ha-me-lin, Ha-me-lin, not long a-go Bruns-wick had no fair-er ci - ty to show

Now you're the smel-li-est town __ in the na - tion be - cause of the Ha - me-lin rat __ oc-cu-pa - tion!

8

Ha-me-lin, Ha-me-lin, we sit and cry,—— your mo - ral stand-ards were al-ways so high,——

Now just be-cause of these ro-dents that plague us,They'd raise a few eye-brows in down - town Las-Ve -

- gas! _____

Ha-me-lin, Ha-me-lin, what's the so-lu-tion To

3. THE RAT RACE RULES
(Eat, Drink and Infest)

* raspberry!

5. AN HOUR THEY SAT

(Mayor and Corporation sit at Council table)

Narrator An hour they sat in coun-cil; At length the Mayor broke si-lence. **Mayor** For a guil-der I'd my er-mine gown sell, I

(colla voce)

Ped. - - - - - - - - - ✱ Ped. - - - - - - - - - ✱

6. THE PIPER'S SONG

7. A CAPITAL FELLOW

8. WE'RE GOING OVER THE WESER

ad lib. quasi recit

Piper When I start to play my pipe I know the mu-sic's com-ing, But I

p (colla voce)

ne-ver know what tune it's going to be, If you come a-long with me you won't

B+5
know where we're go-ing, But you'll fol-low just the same, you'll fol low me.

Am7   D7

[Flute solo]

Cm/Bb

Ped.

Ped.

Slow 4

(Rats begin straggling on, hypnotised)

Slow 4

mp

*or recorder

F♯m/E B7/E
Ha - me-lin was real - ly quite a slum But now the Pi - per
131
E Bm/D
says it's not as hor - ri - ble as some! So blow the bu - gle,
135
C♯7 F♯m Am/F♯ E/B
sound the horn and beat up-on the drum, We're go - ing o - ver the
139
Bsus7 B7 E B7 E
We - - ser! Rats! Rats! hear our bat - tle
144

(They have all marched off)

9. THE PIPER JUST PLAYED

Brisk Jazz Waltz (♩. = 76)

(Re-enter the Rat Leader, soaking wet)

2nd time | Rat Leader | The

Pi - per just played, it sound - ed so rat-ty, It drove us half

bat-ty, we had to sub - mit. We dropped all our nosh, we

left it half swal-lowed, We got up and fol-lowed that

10. YOU SHOULD HAVE HEARD THE HAMELIN PEOPLE

11. YOU'LL HAVE TO REFUSE

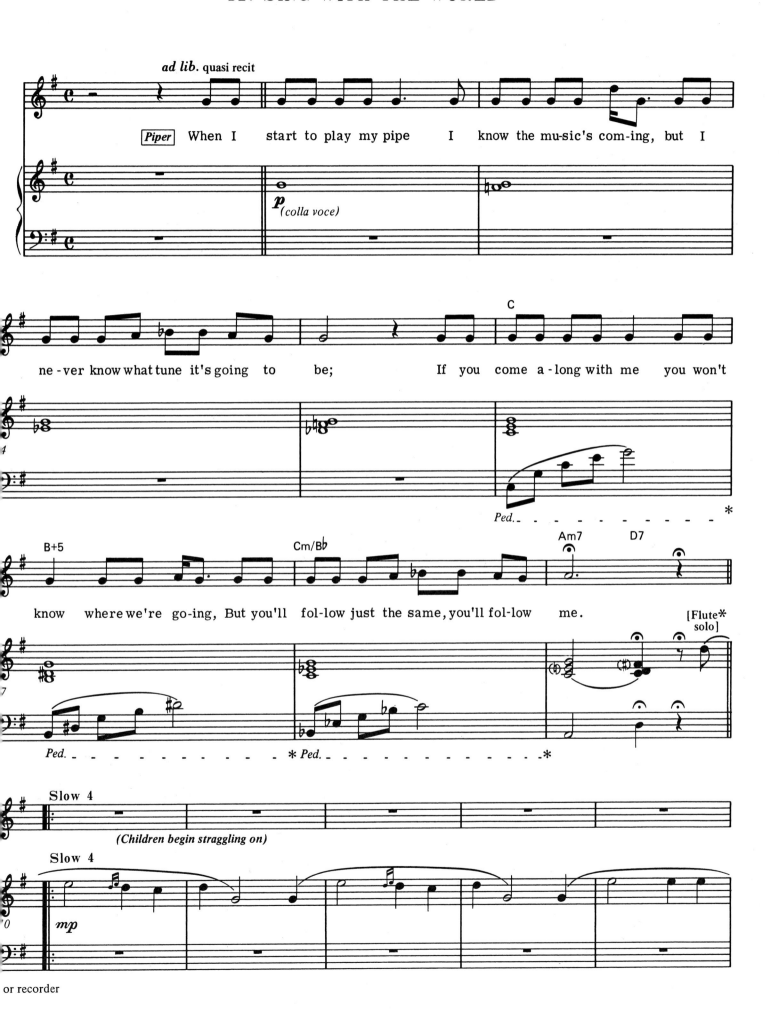

or recorder

Piper There are songs that I know and pla - ces I have been, but let us lis - ten while we're young_ to songs that ne - ver have been sung;_ let us see the pla - ces no - one has e - ver seen._

54

56

13. THE PIPER JUST PLAYED
(Reprise)

60

* or recorder

14. HAMELIN, HAMELIN
(Reprise)

15. A LOST ENDEAVOUR

Narrator (spoken)   But when they saw 'twas a lost endeavour,
And Piper and dancers were gone for ever,
They made a decree that lawyers never
Should think their records dated duly
If, after the day of the month and year,
These words did not as well appear:

"And so long after what happened here
On the Twenty-second of July,
Thirteen Hundred and Seventy Six";
And the better in memory to fix
The place of the Children's last retreat,
They called it the Pied Piper's Street......

(Narrator puts up a sign saying "Pied Piper's Street" and exits.
The Boy comes forward.)

16. WHEN I WAS YOUNG

72

Lyrics:
game _____ when I was young, _____ I dreamt a-
- bout _____ a coun-try far a-way_____ When I was
young, when I was young._____

[Flute Solo]*

*or recorder

17.JUST IN YOUR MIND

(Piper and Children appear in dream-sequence lighting)

80

Printed and bound in Great Britain by
Caligraving Limited Thetford Norfolk